HATTIE'S HOLIDAYS

BOOK 3 OF
THE HATTIE COLLECTION

Marie Hibma Frost

PUBLISHING
Colorado Springs, Colorado

To my sixth grade teacher
who encouraged me to be a writer.

Some Words You May Need to Know

frau	housewife
liefheit	sweetheart
ya	yes
goede morgan	good morning
hockey	a workroom

CONTENTS

Chapter 1

Fun in the Fun House

*H*attie always listened eagerly when Pierce talked about the amusement park at Lake Okoboja.

"I wish you and I could go to the park sometime, Bettie," said Hattie to her good friend Bettie Koostra. Now that Hattie was old enough to go to the Young Peoples Society at church, she often went home with Bettie from the meetings. "Do you like the Ferris wheel?"

"Well, it's kind of scary to be that high in the air," said Bettie.

"Yes," said Hattie, "but it's a fun kind of scared."

Bettie nodded.

"We've just got to find a way to go," continued Hattie. "My dad is always too busy and Mom doesn't drive."

Mrs. Koostra, Bettie's mom, came to the door of the room. She was a typical Dutch *frau*, stoutly built, brisk, and hardworking, but she was also thoughtful and kind.

"I can take you," she said. "I have some shopping to do Saturday in Spirit Lake, and you can go to the park while I'm doing that."

Hattie and Bettie grabbed each other's hands and grinned.

Saturday came, and Hattie, Bettie, and Mrs. Koostra left for the amusement park. "I'll drop you off at the gate, and then I'll pick you up by the Fun House at five this afternoon. Don't keep me waiting. I need to be home in time for supper."

"Let's ride the Ferris wheel first," said Bettie.

"Just so we have enough money left for the Fun House," said Hattie. "When we go in there, we can stay as long as we want."

After they got on the Ferris wheel, the man who operated it continued to load other passengers. Hattie and Bettie moved from one position to the next until they stopped at the very top. There they were, swinging back and forth with their eyes closed. "Do you dare to look down?" Hattie asked Bettie.

"I'll look if you'll look," said Bettie.

They opened their eyes for just a second. They were way above the tops of the trees. They could even see across the lake.

"Oh-h-h-h!" said Hattie. She quickly closed her

eyes again, and Bettie did too. It was frightening to be so high in the air. Soon the Ferris wheel was going round and round, up and down. Hattie held on tight, trying to look straight ahead as the giant wheel went over and over. At last the ride stopped. Hattie staggered a little as she stood up.

"I'm glad we didn't spend any money for a ride on the roller coaster," she laughed. "It goes even higher than the Ferris wheel!"

"We could buy an ice cream cone and still have enough money to go to the Fun House," said Bettie. They had to eat the ice cream quickly. The cones were melting faster in the hot sun than they could lick them.

Finally they headed for the Fun House. It was a very popular place at the park because once you bought a ticket, you could stay inside as long as you wanted to.

"Let's go on the spooky train ride first," said Hattie. "It sounds scary, but it should be fun."

"I won't mind if I can hang on to you," said Bettie, "but I'm afraid to ride on that train."

"Oh, come on," said Hattie. "It'll be fun." The track ran through a tunnel that was black as night. Lights flashed on and off; ghosts and witches jumped out at them. Weird sounds came from every direction. Bettie and Hattie laughed and screamed and screamed and laughed the whole way.

"I didn't know being scared could be so much fun!" admitted Bettie.

The giant slide was their next challenge in the Fun House. They climbed the stairs to a high platform and slid down again and again. "This is almost as scary as the spooky train," said Bettie.

"And as much fun too," added Hattie. "We still have time to go through the barrel." The huge barrel turned round and round. The trick was to walk from one end to the other without falling down while the barrel was turning.

"We're pretty good," said Bettie as they both managed to walk all the way through the barrel.

"Let's do it again," said Hattie.

But this time, they got the giggles, lost their footing, and ended up rolling over and over inside the turning barrel.

In the meantime, Mrs. Koostra was waiting outside the Fun House for them. When they didn't come, the ticket man gave her permission to go in and look for them.

As she walked along the platform looking for the girls, blasts of air would blow up every few seconds through holes in the floor.

"Ooh, ooh," gasped poor Mrs. Koostra with every puff of air. She was doing everything she could to keep her skirt down.

When she got to the entrance to the barrel, she

"Let's do it again," said Hattie.

saw the girls in the middle of the barrel laughing and rolling over and over. She called for them to come, but they couldn't get back on their feet. The barrel seemed to be going faster and faster!

"Those silly girls," she muttered. "Why don't they come when I call them?" There was nothing to do but get them herself.

She was only a step or two inside when she lost her balance and found herself rolling over and over in the barrel!

The little bun of hair at the back of her head began to come loose. She tried to push the hairpins back in with one hand and to hold down her skirt with the other hand—which left her no hands at all to push herself up.

Hattie and Bettie thought having Mrs. Koostra in the barrel was even funnier than being stuck themselves. They began to laugh so hard they could hardly breathe.

But Mrs. Koostra wasn't laughing! "Ooh, ooh, ooh," she panted over and over without stopping. "Oh, my! Oh, dear! Oh, please! Oh, help!" she gasped. Finally she started screaming for the park manager. "Stop this thing!" she yelled in terror.

The ticket man at the entrance realized something was wrong. He quickly pushed the button that stopped the barrel from turning. Mrs. Koostra got to her feet and tried to make herself presentable. "We must go," she said sternly and walked away as quickly as she could.

The girls tried their best to stop their giggles. But all the way home, they had moments when they couldn't hold them in. Mrs. Koostra ignored them. She did not want to hear any more about the fun in the Fun House!

Chapter 2

Ticket Selling at the School Fair

*H*attie was talking with her friend Ruthie Rhenn at recess. "This year would have been more fun if Leonard and Sadie weren't in my class."

"I agree," said Ruthie.

"Leonard has been making trouble for me since the school year started," said Hattie, "and that new girl Sadie is impossible."

"She's pretty, though," said Ruthie.

"Do you like all that rouge she wears on her cheeks?" asked Hattie.

"I don't mind colored cheeks," said Ruthie. "Maybe she is a little stuck up."

"I suppose it's because her dad owns a butcher shop and has enough money to give her almost anything she wants. Sometimes I wish I were the only child," said Hattie.

"Oh, no, don't wish that," said Ruthie. "It's so

lonely to be the only one."

Hattie had to agree. She was glad she had brothers and sisters.

Just then Sadie came by and greeted Hattie with, "Hi, string bean!"

"Hi," said Hattie sweetly. "You should try out for basketball since you're so tall."

"That's a boy's game. I'm not interested," Sadie replied without even looking at Hattie. She walked on without stopping.

"She makes me so mad," said Hattie. "Ever since she didn't get the part of Rose Red, she's been mean to me. She sings almost as well as I do, though. I'm surprised she didn't get the part."

"Maybe her unfriendly attitude had something to do with it," said Ruthie. Then because she didn't really enjoy saying unkind things about anyone, she changed the subject. "Mr. Hinkelman told us to think about ways we can raise money for the school library. You're good at raising money, Hattie. I think he should ask you to help."

Everyone knew the library needed more books. The bookmobile came twice a month, but Harris Elementary School needed its own library. That meant the school needed money to buy books.

As soon as class started, Mr. Hinkelman suggested that the class sponsor a school fair. "We'll need someone to organize it," he said. "Hattie, you have lots of ideas. Why don't you and Ruthie serve as cochairmen?" Ruthie flashed Hattie an I-told-you-so smile. "You two can assign other students to be responsible for different booths," he continued.

Hattie and Ruthie were honored to be chosen to take charge, but it would be a lot of work.

"We'll need some help," said Hattie.

She looked around the class wondering who to ask. Sadie had a scowl on her face. Probably because she hadn't been chosen as chairman.

"Let's have a committee," said Ruthie. "If we ask Sadie, maybe she'll be glad we included her."

"You can ask her," said Hattie. "I don't want to. But I'm going to ask Curtis."

When Ruthie asked Sadie, she was surprised at her response. "I'm not interested in playing second fiddle. If I can't be in charge, I don't want any part of it. I could've run the whole thing myself if Mr. Hinkelman had chosen me."

Curtis, on the other hand, was happy to help. A date was set for the fair and almost everyone was willing to do something.

Cletus volunteered to be in charge of pin the tail on the donkey. Mae wanted to have the booth where people would take turns pitching pennies in a jar. And of course the boys wanted to take charge of the dart games.

Sadie and Lola were in charge of the booth where

people would throw water balloons. Sadie had talked Lola into standing in the tank as the target for the balloons. "I'll collect the money," Sadie offered.

Some of the sixth-grade girls were in charge of the bake sale. Hattie reminded them: "Get as many cakes and loaves of homemade bread as you can. And don't forget the cookies and candy."

Ruthie and Hattie decided they would raffle off a set of dishes donated by Mr. McGowan's Store. Tickets for the raffle would sell for 50¢ apiece. Each ticket had two parts, and the same number was on each part.

After several days had passed, Hattie asked Ruthie, "How are we doing with the sale of the tickets?"

"Not too good," said Ruthie. "Maybe we should have a contest to see who could sell the most raffle tickets."

"Oh, yes," said Hattie. "If we sell enough, we can give the winning salesman a prize like a camera or something."

"That's a great idea," said Ruthie.

They picked out a small box camera at Mr. McGowan's for the prize, and announced the contest.

Hattie sold a lot of tickets. She wanted to buy some herself, but she knew her dad would think she was gambling. There was no gambling allowed for the Hart family.

"I'll just buy one ticket for the good of the cause," said Hattie.

She bought ticket number 99. She didn't want to take it home, so she put it in her desk at school.

The day before the fair, Ruthie and Hattie and their committee were busy decorating the gym. Crepe-paper streamers hung everywhere. Colorful balloons dangled from the light fixtures. They went to get Mr. Hinkelman to see their decorations. But when they came back into the gym, Leonard was stretching the streamers until they dragged on the floor.

"I'll take care of you later, Leonard. Right now go to your classroom and wait for me there," Mr. Hinkelman said.

The girls were ready to cry. "I'll help you pin up the streamers so they won't touch the floor," said Mr. Hinkelman.

When the day of the fair arrived, everyone in town seemed to turn out. The baked goods and candy disappeared immediately. People spent their money at every booth—throwing darts and water balloons, pitching pennies, and eating. The gym was full of happy noise.

Sadie was dressed in her best Sunday clothes. She wore her patent leather shoes and a fancy ribbon in her hair. She was also wearing more rouge than usual. Hattie saw Sadie looking very worried as she ran to the teacher. "Lola isn't coming," said Sadie in alarm. "Who's going to dodge the water balloons?"

"Well, everyone else has a job," said Mr. Hinkelman. "You will just have to do it, I guess."

"And ruin my clothes?" wailed Sadie.

"It's just water," said Mr. Hinkelman, "and you'd better hurry. There are folks lined up at your booth waiting to play right now." Slowly Sadie walked back to her booth.

Two events were saved for the end of the evening: awarding the prize to the top ticket salesman and drawing the winning raffle ticket for the dishes.

Ruthie saw Hattie was busy talking to Mr. Hinkelman. She knew Hattie's ticket was still in her desk, so she ran to the classroom to get it. When she returned, it was time to award the prize to the one who had sold the most tickets. The principal, Mr. Clark, was ready to make the announcement. "The winning salesman is," he paused, "Hattie Hart. She has sold 40 tickets."

Hattie wasn't surprised she had won. She knew she had sold a lot. As she walked up to get her camera, people clapped and cheered.

But as she walked down from the platform, her heart sank. There was her father standing at the doorway of the gym, waiting to take her home. And Hattie couldn't leave until the school fair was over.

After all, she was the chairman.

"Now for the raffle drawing. Do I have a volunteer to pick the winning ticket from the bowl?" asked the principal. Several hands shot up in the air. Then Mr. Clark noticed Sadie looking drenched and forlorn in the back of the room. "Sadie, how would you like to choose our winning ticket?" asked the principal. Sadie, drenched from the water balloons, ran from the gym.

Mr. Clark didn't know what he had done wrong, but quickly called on someone else. Clara was glad to pick the winning ticket. She closed her eyes, reached into the bowl and handed a ticket to Mr. Clark. The principal read the number. "Ninety-nine!" he said in a loud voice. Hattie froze. She had the winning ticket in her desk, but she couldn't claim the prize. It was a good thing it wasn't in her hand. She figured she was already in enough trouble for being the winning raffle salesman.

"Who has the winning ticket?" cried Mr. Clark.

"Here it is!" yelled Ruthie. "I got it from Hattie's desk. It's her ticket."

"Hattie wins the raffle," said Mr. Clark. Between loud cheers and clapping, Hattie stumbled to the platform. How would she ever explain this to Dad? It was bad enough to be the top salesman. But to win the raffle as well!

"How did I ever get into this?" Hattie muttered.

Then she had an idea—maybe she could get herself out of this dilemma by giving the dishes away. She knew Dad would never let her take them home anyway.

"May I say something?" asked Hattie. "Friends were very kind to us a year ago and gave my mother a beautiful set of dishes. I want this prize to go to Lillian Leckban's family." The crowd broke into cheers again. Hattie thought she even saw Dad smile.

Chapter 3

4-H Queen

*M*rs. Miller, the 4-H leader, came to the Harts' house to talk with Hattie about the local 4-H club.

"It's very worthwhile," said Mrs. Miller. "The name of the club stands for four things we try to improve—head, heart, hands, and health. The club encourages young people to take responsibility. Anyone eight years or older can join and then you sign up for a project."

Hattie wasn't interested in taking responsibility, but she was interested in joining a club. "What kind of a project?" she asked.

"Oh, it can be sewing, a handcraft, gardening, or it can be caring for an animal," said Mrs. Miller.

Hattie didn't care much for sewing, handcrafts, or gardening, but an animal project sounded interesting. "What about using Puzzle, my cat?"

"You need to choose," said Mrs. Miller, "some young farm animal such as a pig, lamb, calf, or chickens. You will have to be responsible for it until it is full-grown."

Hattie counted off the possibilities on her fingers. Pig, lamb, calf, or chicken—I choose a pig," she said. "We have lots of those around."

"Rather an unusual choice for a girl," said Mrs. Miller. But she signed Hattie up as a 4-H member.

Hattie could already see herself accepting a blue ribbon for her prize pig at the county fair. She hurried to the barn to ask Dad which pig she could have for her 4-H project.

"The only one I can spare," said Dad, "is that little one over there." He pointed at the saddest, skinniest little runt of a pig Hattie had ever seen.

"Oh, Dad, not that one! He'll never, ever win a prize!"

"Listen, Hattie, if you take good care of him, you'll be surprised. Right now he doesn't get enough milk, because he's crowded away from his mother by the other pigs."

Hattie got an old medicine dropper from Dad and started dripping milk into her skinny little pig's mouth. First she pretended the pig was a baby who needed to be fed. Then she pretended he was a very sick patient in the hospital and she was a nurse saving his life.

After a few extra feedings she was tired of pretending. "You certainly eat often enough," she said to her pig as she put him down. He had enough energy to make his way back to his mother.

At the next 4-H meeting, Mrs. Miller announced there would be tryouts for a 4-H queen. "Any member ten years or over is eligible," she said.

That means I am eligible, said Hattie to herself.

"You will be judged," continued Mrs. Miller, "on character, charm, and appearance. A girl from each club in the county will compete."

Hattie started laying her plans. For a long time, she had wanted to wear glasses. *It will make me look older and more dignified,* she thought.

She took a pair of Mom's old wire-rimmed glasses and began wearing them, even though the lenses were missing. *I have to do something about my hair too.* She'd seen a picture in a magazine at school of a movie actress who had long blonde hair with bangs. She began combing her hair toward the front of her face.

"You look like a sheep that needs shearing," said her brother Pierce. "And take those glasses off. They don't help your looks one bit."

Hattie ignored him. She knew she had charm and character. And she had improved her appearance so she had a chance to win.

There was one problem—Mrs. Miller, the leader, had picked her own daughter, Caroline, to be the candidate to represent the local club.

"It's not fair," Hattie told her mother. "She's fat and dumpy, and she has no personality whatsoever.

25

She will never be picked as the county queen."

The place of judging was at the Harris High School gym a week before the county fair. Judging would begin at one o'clock. Hattie wore her red dress and glasses even though she was not to compete.

As each girl came onto the platform, she was supposed to walk around and talk to the others. The judges would observe her and make their decisions.

Poor Caroline was standing stiffly in one spot. "Hattie," Mrs. Miller whispered, "Go to the platform. Talk to Caroline and get her to walk around. Tell her to smile too. I know you can help her relax."

Hattie went up on the platform and did as Mrs. Miller had requested. She took Caroline's hand and introduced her to some of the girls. She succeeded in getting Caroline to move around and smile as Hattie happily chatted away. Hattie was so carried away with her role that she helped other girls too.

Meanwhile, the judges were carefully observing what was happening. After some time had passed, they handed their ballots to the chairman of the judging committee.

"We have noticed an error," said one of the judges. "The name of the girl we have chosen is missing from the list of candidates."

There was an awkward silence.

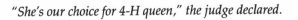

"She's our choice for 4-H queen," the judge declared.

"What is the name of the tall blonde girl wearing a red dress and glasses?" the judge asked.

Suddenly, everyone was looking at Hattie. She was the only one wearing glasses and a red dress.

Mrs. Miller got to her feet to protest. "The girl's name is Hattie Hart, but she wasn't supposed to be a candidate," she said.

The judges insisted. "She's our choice for 4-H queen," the head judge declared.

Some of the girls tried to smile at Hattie, even though they were disappointed not to have been chosen. Caroline walked down the stairs looking sideways at Hattie. She wasn't smiling.

I suppose she thinks I planned it all, said Hattie to herself.

Mrs. Miller said nothing, since she was the one who had Hattie go to the stage. The judges came up on the platform to congratulate Hattie.

"You're a winner," said one of the judges. "You should go far in life."

A winner? thought Hattie. *I'm on my way to fame and fortune.*

Chapter 4

Prizewinning Pumpkin

*I*t was getting close to time for the county fair, and Hattie could hardly wait. This year she knew she would win a prize. She had been working on it since last spring.

It had all started when Mom planted lots of pumpkin vines in her garden. They had just begun to peek out of the ground when Hattie asked, "Mom, may I choose one of the vines? I'd like to enter the pumpkin contest at the fair." Each year at the county fair there was competition to see who had grown the largest pumpkin.

"If she's going to be in a contest, I'm going to be in one too," said Clarence.

"Hey!" said Pierce, "you can't leave me out of this. I can beat Hattie any day!"

"Hattie will win. She always does," said little Leona.

And that's how the competition began. Pierce,

Hattie, and Clarence had all rushed to the garden to stake out their claim.

First Pierce picked out a vine along the edge of the garden.

"I'll find a stick and drive it in the ground and tie my bandanna on it," he said. "Then everyone will know it's mine."

"I found the vine I want," said Clarence. "I'm going to put a big stone by mine for a marker."

Hattie took her time making a choice.

"North, south, east, west, show me which one is the best," she chanted as she closed her eyes and twirled around three times. When she opened her eyes, her finger was pointing to one in the corner. "I don't need a marker," she said. "I can remember."

Every day the three of them checked their vines. The race was on.

"Oh, look," said Hattie. "The vines have started spreading." Soon, bell-shaped blossoms appeared all along the vines.

Hattie wanted to know all about how to grow pumpkins, and she knew Ruthie's mother had a garden book.

"May I borrow your book, Mrs. Rhenn?" Hattie asked.

"Why, of course," Ruthie's mom said. She was glad to help.

Hattie had her nose in that book all afternoon.

She learned several secrets about how to grow larger pumpkins.

"I'm watering mine every day," bragged Pierce. Hattie didn't tell him that the book warned, "Don't get water on the leaves."

Soon the blossoms were gone and in their places were little green pumpkins. As the pumpkins grew, Clarence and Hattie kept checking to see who had the biggest pumpkin.

I know how I can make my pumpkin grow faster, said Hattie to herself. *I'll do what the book says, but I'll keep it a secret.*

That evening, after her brothers had gone to bed, Hattie took a lantern, a small bucket, and a small shovel. She slipped out to the barn and went to the manure pile in back.

"Yuck!" said Hattie as she scooped some manure in the bucket. "I sure hate doing this, but if I want to win, I've got to fertilize my pumpkin."

Every few days for several weeks, Hattie was out in the dark taking care of her pumpkin. She watched it grow bigger and bigger.

Mine's lots bigger than either Pierce's or Clarence's, she decided. *I think I've got a winner.*

Clarence and Pierce were puzzled. It seemed that all Hattie had to do was look at her pumpkin and it grew.

One evening when Mom was in the kitchen, she

looked out the window and saw a light moving near the barn.

"You'd better go, Nick," she said to Dad, "and see who is prowling around the barn. Maybe it's chicken thieves!"

Dad hurried to the barn to see what was going on.

"Who's there?" he yelled.

Hattie was so startled, she dropped her bucket.

"Whatever are you doing in the manure pile?" asked Dad.

"I'm helping my pumpkin grow," said Hattie. "But don't tell Pierce and Clarence."

"O.K.," Dad laughed. "I'll keep your secret."

It was the day before the fair was to start. The pumpkins had long since turned orange. Hattie's was by far the biggest.

The whole family came to look. They stood around, admiring her pumpkin.

"It beats me," said Pierce, "how you always come out ahead. No sense in Clarence and me taking ours to the fair."

Tomorrow Hattie would take her prize pumpkin to the fair. She knew she'd be the winner and get a blue ribbon and a prize of two dollars.

The next morning Hattie went to the garden to check on her pumpkin.

"Oh, no!" screamed Hattie. "The stem is broken off! Who ruined my pumpkin? You have to have a stem to enter the competition!" She burst into tears.

The family came running to see what was the trouble.

"Who did this? Who broke the stem off Hattie's pumpkin?" asked Dad sternly as he looked at each of the children.

Leona was crying. She knew she had done something wrong. "I just tried to lift it and the stem came off in my hand," sobbed Leona.

Hattie felt so sorry when she saw Leona crying that she couldn't say much to her. Neither could Dad.

"Mine's pretty big. Maybe I should enter mine," said Pierce.

"All right, Pierce," said Dad. "You'd better load your pumpkin in the wagon. Is everybody ready?"

Later that day Pierce came home with a blue ribbon and two dollars. "Here Hattie, this belongs to you," he said. "Your pumpkin would have been the winner."

"No," said Hattie. "I was selfish. I didn't want you or Clarence to win. I should have shared my secrets for growing a big pumpkin with you."

"Well," said Pierce. "Maybe we should split the two dollars." And so they did.

Chapter 5

Mashed Potatoes with Gravy

om was the stay-at-home kind. *What else can Mom do?* thought Hattie. *She has five children at home and that keeps her busy!*

The day before Thanksgiving, Dad came up with what he thought was a brilliant idea. "Why don't we invite the Orange City relatives over for Thanksgiving dinner," he said. Orange City was about fifty miles from the Harts' farm.

"Nick!" Mom said in alarm. She always called him that when she was very serious. "I can barely make dinner for our own family. On such short notice, I could never prepare food for forty more people."

"I don't think forty people will be able to come," Dad said. "Anyway, we can ask them to bring their

Thanksgiving dinners along. We will have plenty of food."

"I don't know," said Mom anxiously.

"The girls can help," continued Dad.

While Mom and Dad were trying to work out an agreement, Hattie thought about all the relatives who might come. *Let's see now. I like Aunt Rica and Uncle Sip and their kids. You can tell Aunt Rica likes kids.*

Then Hattie thought of Uncle Ted, the minister. *He always preaches, even when he's just talking to you. But I'd like to see Cousin Arnetta. My favorite uncle is Uncle Garrett. He's a bachelor. He laughs a lot and is always smiling.*

And then Hattie thought of her very least favorite aunt, Aunt Minnie. None of the children in the family liked her. She never invited any of the children to her house because she was afraid they would ruin her fine things. Worst of all, whenever she saw Hattie, she always said the same thing: "Little Hattie, how you have grown!" *Doesn't she know that I'm not little, and everybody grows!* thought Hattie.

Early the next morning Mom made an urgent plea. "I'll have to have help if the relatives are coming, Hattie. You can start peeling the potatoes right away! Dad has called and there are at least thirty-two people coming. And Hattie," said Mom sternly, "don't you make trouble!"

"What do you mean?" asked Hattie innocently.

"You have good intentions, liefheit, but sometimes your ideas are not so good," Mom explained.

Hattie started peeling potatoes in earnest—lots of potatoes. Mom was famous for her mashed potatoes. They were creamy and buttery and oh, so fluffy. "Adding a little pinch of baking powder does the trick, Hattie," she said. Hattie pledged never to tell Mom's secret.

The potatoes finally were cooking on the stove. While Hattie set the table, she sang over and over again a song she had learned at school. Only Hattie made up different words to fit the tune. She sang at the top of her lungs:

Over the river and through the woods,
The Hart relatives go.
Some I like and some I don't,
And some I barely know.

Suddenly Mom warned, "Hattie, the company's here! Three carloads of them." Flustered, Mom rushed to the kitchen to check on the turkey. She was glad she had put it in the oven early and that it was a big one!

Dad opened the door and people came streaming in, their arms full of sweet potato casseroles, stuffing

Suddenly Mom warned, "Hattie, the company's here!"

casseroles, cheese casseroles, applesauce, cranberries, relishes, preserves, all kinds of pickles—pickled beans, pickled beets, pickled cucumbers, even pickled watermelon—and of course the mincemeat and pumpkin pies.

Uncle Garrett was the only one who greeted Hattie with a big hug. The cousins all started talking at once, and soon Hattie and Arnetta were off in a corner, talking by themselves.

Uncle Sip's two little children kept hanging on to him, one on each leg. Hattie wondered if they did that all the time. If so, how could Uncle Sip walk? *Maybe he waddles,* Hattie thought.

Hattie saw Aunt Minnie out of the corner of her eye, and pretended she hadn't seen her. But Aunt Minnie saw Hattie!

"How are you, little Hattie," she said sweetly and loudly. "My, how little Hattie has grown." Just what Hattie had expected her to say! Hattie didn't bother to answer.

After everybody had gotten acquainted again, Dad announced, "Dinner is ready!" Soon they were seated at the big dining room table. Dad had added extra leaves so everyone could sit down at the same time. The table was crowded with food. The glistening brown turkey sat on a platter at one end, ready for Dad to carve.

Mom brought out hot green beans, fresh

homemade bread, more pickles and jams, and of course a large bowl of mashed potatoes, fluffy and dotted with butter. Next to it she set a bowl of rich brown gravy.

"Let's pray," said Dad.

"When Uncle Ted prays, the food gets cold," Hattie whispered to Uncle Garrett, who sat next to her. He smiled and gave her a knowing look.

Dad's prayer was short, but beautiful. He sounded so grateful to God that everyone else felt grateful too. His words made Hattie think of all the good things she could be thankful for—Mom and Dad, brothers, sisters who loved her, and God, who took care of them all. She was especially thankful God kept forgiving her for all the bad things she did.

While Dad carved the turkey, people started passing other dishes around the table. There was only one thing that worried Hattie. As the potatoes were being passed, they were rapidly disappearing. There were no more in the kitchen, and several of the people at the table hadn't been served yet. Hattie thought of a secret the family often shared when company was present. Whenever Mom said "M-I-K," it meant "more in kitchen." If she said, "F-H-B," it meant "family hold back."

However, Mom was too busy to realize what was happening. She was trying to quiet little Ervin and, at the same time, keep the coffee cups filled. Hattie could see that Aunt Minnie, seated at the far end of the table, would be the last person to have the potatoes passed to her. Next to Aunt Minnie sat Pierce. He looked at Hattie, wondering if there were enough potatoes left for him and Aunt Minnie.

"M-I-K," said Hattie loudly to Pierce. She really didn't know why she said that, except that she didn't like Aunt Minnie and didn't care if she got any potatoes or not. Hattie knew there weren't any more potatoes, and she knew she should have said "F-H-B." Then Pierce wouldn't have taken all the potatoes left in the bowl.

Mom, holding little Ervin in one arm, picked up the empty bowl to refill it in the kitchen. But there were no more potatoes!

"Ya, I'm sorry, Minnie," said Mom. "I should have cooked more potatoes." Trying to hide her embarrassment, she said, "Pass Aunt Minnie some vegetables and turkey."

"No, thank you," Aunt Minnie said crisply. "I usually eat potatoes with my turkey."

"Do you want some extra gravy?" offered Aunt Rica.

"Hardly," said Aunt Minnie. "What good is gravy without potatoes?"

Pierce and other members of the family looked at the mounds of potatoes still on their plates and felt embarrassed. They didn't know what to do. After all, they had already started eating.

But Hattie knew what to do. All of a sudden, she felt sorry for Aunt Minnie. Aunt Minnie must sense that most of the children didn't like her, including Hattie. She had been mean to tell Pierce "M-I-K" when it wasn't true. Hattie had been so busy talking, she hadn't touched her food. On her plate was still a big mound of potatoes. Hattie got up from her chair, picked up her plate, and put it in front of Aunt Minnie.

"I want you to have these," said Hattie. "I haven't eaten any of them yet, and I'd rather save room for Mom's lemon pie."

Aunt Minnie started to protest, but Hattie had already left the table, offering to hold Ervin for Mom so she would have a chance to eat.

"What an adorable child!" said Aunt Minnie as her fork dipped into Mom's fluffy potatoes.

Maybe I'll learn to like Aunt Minnie after all, she thought.

Mom, before sitting down at the table, whispered in Hattie's ear, "Thank you, Hattie. It's nice to have someone to count on when we have company."

Hattie felt good all over. Just this once, it was better than Mom's potatoes.

Chapter 6

The Music Teacher

*H*attie liked music, but she didn't like her music teacher. Miss Newell wore straight, plain dresses that were usually covered with chalk dust. She was crabby, and she believed that music was all business and no fun. One boy hated the class so much that he hid in the bathroom when it was time for music.

Miss Newell began every class with, "All right, children, let's get ready for our warm-up exercises. We must have a relaxed throat to sing properly." Hattie wasn't interested in a relaxed throat. Hattie just wanted to sing.

Miss Newell wanted everyone in the class to sing a solo. Ah-ah-ah-ah and Ooh-ooh-ooh, up and down the scales they sang.

Tired of singing the scales, Arnold asked, "Can't we sing 'Coming 'Round the Mountain'?"

"I was hired to teach you to sing proper songs,"

said Miss Newell. "Now, shall we begin singing Brahms Lullaby again?"

"We've been singing that every day for a month," said Hattie. "Can't we sing something new?"

"After we have learned Brahms Lullaby," said Miss Newell sternly.

Hattie was sure something had to be done about Miss Newell and her music class. She talked over her problem with Mom that evening.

"We are all miserable in her music class," complained Hattie.

"I can't be responsible for the others," said Mom, "but it would be nice if you did something to help Miss Newell. She's a lonely maiden lady, and music is the love of her life."

That gave Hattie an idea. If she didn't want Miss Newell to be crabby, she needed to find someone to be the love of her life instead of music.

The next day Hattie asked Arnold what to do.

"Who in the world could we find who would like Miss Crab, I mean Miss Newell," Arnold said.

"There's got to be someone who will like her," said Hattie.

"It would be easier to quit singing than to like her," said Arnold. "Ever since she told me not to sing, just to move my lips, I hate her!"

"That was dumb," said Hattie, "but she probably did it because you can't sing." Hattie's mind was racing ahead. "I just thought of a perfect boyfriend. There's a man in our church, you know, Henry Post!"

"But," interrupted Arnold, "isn't he too old? Miss Newell is about 40, and I think Henry is about 60."

"That's not too bad," said Hattie. "We can't be too picky."

The next Sunday, Hattie put her plan into action.

"This was just a get-acquainted time," explained Hattie. "It's only the beginning. I have other ideas too."

The following Sunday, Hattie once again sought out Henry.

"Would you do me a favor, Henry?" Hattie asked innocently. "We have a teacher who is very sad. I'm trying to make her happy, but I don't want her to think I'm trying to be a teacher's pet. Would you stop by her house and give her this?" Hattie handed him a small package. "If she asks who it is from, just say, 'Guess who!' Then she won't know it's from me."

Henry wondered what Hattie was doing, but he wanted to do whatever he could to help any of the Harts. They were good to invite him to dinner so often; and Hattie was a nice girl to want to help her teacher.

So the next night Henry knocked on Miss Newell's door. He was greeted not by Miss Newell, but by a man!

"What can I do for you?" he asked.

"Would you please give this to Miss Newell?" Henry said. "Just say it's from 'Guess who'."

The man stared at Mr. Post. "You'd better take your gift and get out of here before I punch you in the nose," said the man angrily. "I'm her husband and I don't appreciate other men making advances toward my wife."

Poor Henry! He ran as fast as he could. He wasn't looking for anyone to punch him in the nose.

The next day at school, Miss Newell announced, "Some of you may not know that I'm married because you have never met my husband."

Hattie thought Miss Newell looked right at her when she said that.

Miss Newell knew that the school board liked to hire only unmarried or widowed ladies as teachers. The board thought that someone with a husband or a family wouldn't have time to be a good teacher. And Miss Newell hadn't wanted anyone to find out she was married.

"You may still call me Miss Newell," she told the class.

Arnold stopped Hattie at lunch. "Next time you ask me to help, get your facts straight," he scolded. "You sure embarrassed poor Henry."

"I only wanted to help, so Miss Newell wouldn't be so crabby."

"I have an idea," said Ruthie, who had joined Hattie for lunch. "Let's give Miss Newell an apple shower." Apple showers were traditional at the Harris Elementary School.

"Why didn't I think of that?" said Hattie.

The next Friday, everyone in Hattie's class had their pockets bulging with shiny red apples for Miss Newell.

"When I give the signal," said Arnold, "roll your apples down the aisle."

When it was time for music class, Miss Newell made her way to the front of the room. Arnold tapped his pencil on his desk. Suddenly a torrent of apples came thumping and bumping down the aisle. Poor Miss Newell shrieked and backed against the desk and slowly slid to the floor.

"Run! Get the principal!" shouted Hattie. "Something terrible has happened to Miss Newell!"

The principal came running into the room. By then, Miss Newell had opened her eyes and was sitting up.

"Here, let me help you," said Mr. Clark. He saw all the apples on the floor and guessed what had happened. He smiled at Miss Newell as he helped her to her feet, "You've had an apple shower. The class was only trying to show how much they love you."

Miss Newell stood up and for the first time, they saw her smile a real smile.

"And now," said Miss Newell, once the class had helped her pick up the apples, "Let's start by singing one of your favorite songs. What will it be?"

"Let's sing, 'She'll Be Coming 'Round the Mountain When She Comes'!" said Hattie.

Even Miss Newell joined in the singing.

Chapter 7

Aunt Hattie's Hat

*O*n the first Saturday in December, the weather hovered between fall and winter. A cold, gray rain started and stopped and started again.

"Nasty weather," said Dad as he came in from the barn. It's a good day to stay in and read a book. I don't know if Aunt Hattie and Uncle John will come tomorrow to celebrate Hattie's birthday or not. This rain may change to snow."

Minutes later Hattie saw a car coming in the driveway. Aunt Hattie and Uncle John had arrived a day early.

"Goede morgan," said Mom. She held the door as Uncle John and Aunt Hattie came in, shaking off the rain.

Whenever Aunt Hattie came to visit, Mom would ask, "May I take your hat and coat for you?"

"My coat, please, Anna," Aunt Hattie would

answer. "But I'll keep my hat on."

Aunt Hattie never came to visit without wearing her hat. It was a funny little hat made of soft felt. It had a small brim and a little red flower in the front. The Hart children were intrigued by Aunt Hattie's hat.

Hattie was named for her aunt. She liked Aunt Hattie, but not her name. She tried to think of another name that would still be loyal to her Aunt Hattie. She thought of Harriet and Heather and also of using her middle name: Marie H. or H. Marie. In the end, she always came back to plain old Hattie.

"Here's a present for my birthday girl," said Aunt Hattie. She handed Hattie a little wooden box with a gold latch.

"It's beautiful," said Hattie looking at the box.

"There's something inside too," said Aunt Hattie.

What could Aunt Hattie have possibly put in the box? Hattie opened the lid, and there, wrapped in pink tissue paper, was the most beautiful handkerchief she had ever seen. It was bordered with fine lace and had pink ribbon woven into the edge. The letter H had been embroidered in one corner.

Hattie carefully took the handkerchief from the box. As she did, out rolled some pennies. Hattie knew she had found them all when she counted ten because she was ten years old.

"Thank you! Thank you!" said Hattie. "I will keep my handkerchief just for Sundays. And I'll buy you a present with the money you gave me."

"That won't be necessary," said Aunt Hattie. "I'm just glad you like your present."

"Can you stay for the day?" asked Mom.

"Maybe we can stay for lunch," said Aunt Hattie, looking at her husband. "John wants to go back soon in case it starts to snow. We didn't want to miss Hattie's birthday, but this is a busy time at the grain elevator."

Aunt Hattie and Uncle John worked at the farmers elevator in the nearby town of Sibley. They didn't have any children.

"Maybe Hattie would like to stay with us for a few days?" offered Aunt Hattie.

Hattie was tempted, but she knew she couldn't go. "I would like to come with you—very much— but Mom needs my help," apologized Hattie.

Aunt Hattie's crooked little smile and twinkling eyes looked disappointed. "Well, I hope some other time," she said.

During lunch, all the Hart children were watching Aunt Hattie's hat and wondering why she never took it off.

After Aunt Hattie and Uncle John had said good-by and Hattie had thanked them again for the lovely handkerchief, everyone came back in the dining room where Dad was sitting by the heater.

They were still thinking about Aunt Hattie's hat and why she never took it off.

"Maybe she doesn't have any hair and doesn't want us to find out about it," said Clarence.

"Maybe her hair is growed to her hat," suggested Leona.

Hattie was sure she was hiding a rare string of heirloom pearls that had belonged to her grandmother.

"If you promise never to tell anyone—especially Aunt Hattie," said Dad, "I will tell you a story about the day Aunt Hattie's hat came off."

"We promise, we promise," they chorused.

"Well," started Dad slowly, "One day—"

"Hurry up, Dad," interrupted Hattie.

"Be quiet, Hattie," said Clarence.

Dad waited for silence and went on. "Mom invited Aunt Hattie to come and see how much work we had done to make the hockey look nice. We had fixed it up so the hired man could sleep there. There was a new heater and some new curtains and things that ladies usually like to look at.

"But Aunt Hattie was in a hurry. Uncle John never wants to stay too long—like today. So she and Mom were walking pretty quickly. As they came across the yard, Aunt Hattie didn't see the clothesline. It caught her hat and flipped it off her head. All of a sudden," Dad paused, "the air was full of paper money!

"Aunt Hattie started yelling, 'Help! My money! It's blowing away!'

"Your mom and Aunt Hattie ran all over the yard to find the money. And they weren't one dollar bills. They were one-hundred-dollar bills!

"When all the money was picked up and back in Aunt Hattie's hands, she just stood there looking embarrassed. Finally she said, 'Well, I guess my secret's out.'"

"Dad, is that a true story?" asked Hattie.

"I was just coming in from the barn and I saw the whole thing," said Dad. "Everybody knows Aunt Hattie doesn't trust banks."

"Come on, Dad," said Pierce, not satisfied. "Where would she get all that money?"

"Maybe Aunt Hattie was named after a rich aunt who gave her all her money when she died," said Hattie brightly.

"What are you thinking, Hattie?" Dad asked with a smile.

"I may have to wear a hat someday," Hattie replied.

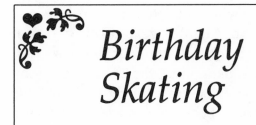

Chapter 8

Birthday Skating

*T*oday was Hattie's birthday. Hattie was growing up, but she wasn't sure she wanted to.

Growing up is confusing, Hattie thought as she rode the bus to school. *Sometimes I feel older than Pierce, and sometimes I feel younger than Clarence. Sometimes people make fun of me because I still like to play with dolls. They think I'm strange because every once in a while I still cry. It's hard to grow up. And people keep telling me, "Act your age, Hattie." What really is my age? I feel all mixed up inside.*

"What's the matter, droopy?" asked Arnold. "Don't you know it takes fewer muscles to smile than it does to frown?" Arnold was pleased to share this new piece of information.

Hattie nodded. She wanted to smile more than anything. After all, anyone who wasn't happy on her birthday must be a little strange. *I'll just choose to be happy,* Hattie thought with determination.

Soon Hattie and Arnold were talking about getting older, about all the challenges and adventures waiting just around the bend. The more they talked, the better Hattie felt. By the time she got to school, she was beginning to feel good about her birthday.

Just before lunchtime, there was a knock on the door.

"May I speak to Hattie?" asked a familiar voice.

Hattie hurried to the door, and there stood Mom holding a cake.

"For your birthday, Hattie, to share with your classmates," said Mom. "And here's some cold lemonade too."

"Oh, Mom, I love you," said Hattie. "Thank you! Thank you!"

"Ya, ya," Mom said with a little smile. Her face was red and she left in a hurry.

Hattie marched back into the room holding the birthday cake.

"It's time to celebrate Hattie's birthday," said the teacher. Everyone pushed their books and papers aside for a party, and then they sang Happy Birthday to Hattie.

The cake was a yellow sponge cake with white frosting and coconut sprinkled on top. Hattie wondered why the cake wasn't chocolate—her favorite.

As they munched on cake, Ruthie handed Hattie a package. Hattie quickly unwrapped it. It was a blue stocking cap, scarf, and mittens.

"Oh, my," said Hattie, beaming with surprise.

"I helped Mom knit them," said Ruthie proudly. "We wanted you to have a whole matching set."

"They're beautiful," Hattie said. "Thank you, Ruthie."

Arnold had put a small package on Hattie's desk. It was a wooden horse, carved by hand.

"I thought it might make you think of riding Topsy," said Arnold shyly.

"Thank you, Arnold," Hattie said. "It even looks like Topsy!"

Lillian gave Hattie six cornbread cupcakes. "I'll eat one for lunch and take the rest home for my birthday supper," said Hattie. "Thank you, Lillian. You make the best cornbread in the world."

By the time Hattie reached home, she felt like she'd already celebrated her birthday.

The whole family wanted to make Hattie's birthday special. Clarence made place cards. Leona set the table with Mom's best white dishes for twelve. Mom had cooked all of Hattie's favorite foods—fried chicken, mashed potatoes and gravy, sweet corn, and apple salad.

After a second helping of fluffy mashed potatoes,

Clarence said, "This supper is great! I wish somebody had a birthday every day!"

"We'd all get fat!" laughed Dad.

"Well, maybe I should bring the dessert a little later then," said Mom.

After Dad said a special prayer for Hattie, she opened her presents. Hattie loved surprises. And every package was more of a surprise.

Ervin had colored a picture to give to Hattie. "Leona helped me," he said.

Leona gave Hattie a card that said she would wash dishes for Hattie all week.

Kathryn and Lawrence had sent Hattie a rhinestone barrette for her hair. "It looks like real diamonds," said Hattie.

Hattie wondered if Mom had forgotten to give her a gift.

"See the string under your plate?" said Pierce. "Pull it out and read the note that's attached to it."

Hattie read:

Follow this string wherever it goes,
It leads to your present but no one knows,
How useful they'll be when the cold wind blows.

Hattie wondered if it would be a pair of boots or a new winter jacket.

Quickly she traced the string to the reservoir on

the back of the stove. There, lying on the stove was a shining silver key with another note attached:

> *Behind the stove,*
> *You will see,*
> *Something I wish was meant for me.*
> *Put them on your two big feet.*
> *I'm sure that you'll enjoy the treat!*

"Ice skates!" screamed Hattie as she reached behind the stove. There was the most beautiful pair of skates she'd ever seen! They were so shiny they looked like real silver.

"Oh, thank you, Mom! Thank you, Dad! Thank you, Pierce!" Pierce had helped Mom and Dad buy the skates for Hattie, and he also had composed the poems.

"I checked the pond in the pasture across the fence and it's thick enough for skating. We'll go tomorrow," said Pierce.

"When are we going to eat the birthday cake?" asked Leona.

"Right now," said Mom. She went to the pantry and brought out a cake with dark chocolate frosting and pink candles.

Now it was time for the family to sing Happy Birthday. Hattie loved the way her family sang together.

But Hattie was so excited about her skates that, for once, she barely tasted her favorite cake.

Finally the party was over. Dishes were all washed and the younger children were in bed. Clarence and Pierce were upstairs playing checkers. Dad was in the living room in his favorite chair, reading. Mom had gone to bed early to try to get little Ervin to sleep.

Hattie was alone in the kitchen. *Today was the most wonderful day of my life,* she thought. She tried on her skates. They fit perfectly. She glanced out the window. There was a full moon that gave enough light to go skating.

Without any more thought, she took off her skates and grabbed her coat and boots. Even though she knew she wasn't supposed to go out alone at night, especially in cold weather, she pulled on her cap and mittens. She slipped quietly out the kitchen door, her skates tucked under her arms.

She quickly made her way to the pond and sat down to put on her new skates. They were so white and pretty in the moonlight.

"What a beautiful night for skating!" said Hattie as she started moving out on the ice. Soon she was gliding smoothly over the ice. As she skated she thought of a poem.

God's big bright moon

Above my head,
I'm glad I'm skating and not in bed.
Then I would miss your silvery sheen
Shining on this winter scene.

And then it happened! Her skate caught on the end of a tree branch sticking up out of the ice. In a split second, Hattie felt herself spinning around. She lost her balance and crashed down hard on the ice.

Something snapped in her ankle, and she felt a stabbing pain. She was sure she had broken her ankle. She tried to stand up, but she couldn't. It hurt too much.

"What do I do now?" cried Hattie. "If I stay out here, I'll freeze to death, but I can't walk. I guess I'll have to crawl."

Hattie got on her hands and knees and crawled toward the fence. Her fingers and toes were so cold they felt numb. She struggled through the snow until she came to the fence.

A hundred thoughts raced through her head. How will I ever climb over the fence with a broken ankle? No one knows I'm out here. No one will come looking for me. Maybe I'll freeze to death. I'll die on my birthday.

"Please, dear God," she prayed aloud, "send someone to help me."

Just then she saw a light. It was her father,

carrying a lantern. He was on his way to the barn to check on a new calf that had looked sick earlier that evening.

"Dad! Help me!" yelled Hattie.

But Dad didn't hear her and the lantern disappeared in the barn.

"Dear God," Hattie prayed once again, "if I'm going to die, please forgive me for all the bad things I've done. I keep telling You I'm sorry and I won't be bad anymore, but then I forget and I'm bad all over again. I know You still love me, and You can give me a new heart." Hattie felt peaceful. In heaven, she wouldn't have to work at being good. She would be as sweet and kind and cheerful as Ruthie or her sister Kathryn ever thought about being.

Hattie was so cold she began to feel sleepy. She saw a light in the distance. Maybe it was the light of angels coming for her. Soon she'd be in heaven.

A light! She tried to pull herself up. It wasn't angels, it was her father on his way back to the house.

She yelled with all that was left of her might, "Dad, help, help!"

This time, Dad heard her. He dropped his lantern, and ran in the moonlight toward the pasture fence, and almost leaped over it. There lay Hattie, so cold she couldn't lift her arms as Dad reached down to pick her up. "Oh, little fanka, I hope I found you in time," he said as he carried her back to the house.

"Anna, quick!" he called to Mom. "Open the door. It's Hattie. She's hurt and half-frozen to death."

Dad laid Hattie on the couch. Mom started rubbing Hattie's arms and legs. "Ach, my fanka, you are so cold." Hattie moaned when Mom rubbed her leg.

"She's hurt," said Dad, trying to stay calm. "I'll call Dr. Broden!"

"Hattie, Hattie," said Mom with tears in her eyes, "why did you go out to the pond by yourself?"

Hattie's head was clearing. She was so glad to be back in the house where it was warm. She didn't care about much else—except her ankle.

"Oh, Mom, my ankle hurts so bad." Hattie grabbed Mom's hand. She had never had anything hurt as much as her ankle did now. She could hardly speak. "Mom, I'm sorry I went out alone. I know I wasn't supposed to. Please forgive me. I'll never do it again."

"Ya, we forgive you," said Mom. "But you need to rest now. The doctor will be here soon. He'll take care of your ankle."

Dr. Broden confirmed that Hattie's ankle was badly broken.

"I'll put a temporary splint on it tonight and tomorrow we'll put on a cast. Soon it will be good as new."

"God has been good to us," said Dad. "You could

have frozen to death out there."

"And on my birthday too," said Hattie.

"God must have many more birthdays in mind for you," said Dad. "I think He needs people like you in this world who don't give up."

"I think," said Hattie sleepily, "He needs people who will listen to Him."

Blizzard

*I*t was a gray Wednesday. Hattie tried to listen as Miss Henry explained long division, but she couldn't help looking out the window. Hattie was sharing her desk with Leona today. Sometimes Leona got to visit the school with Hattie even though she wasn't old enough to be in her own class. Watching little Leona color a picture was more interesting to Hattie than Miss Henry's arithmetic lesson.

At least, tomorrow was Saturday. *If only it would snow*, thought Hattie, *I know Pierce would take me sledding.* As if in answer to her wish, a snowflake drifted by the window. Hattie began saying softly to herself, "Snow, snow, more snow, then a-sledding we can go!"

As the day went by, more snow fell. Big, soft, quiet flakes were whirling and spinning down from the sky.

Even Miss Henry looked out of the schoolroom window. Once the snow stopped, only to start again. Dark clouds were rolling out of the northwest, blotting out the sun. About two o'clock, Mr. Clark, the principal, came into the room and announced, "The bus will be leaving in a few minutes."

The class hurried into their winter wraps, glad that school was out early. Hattie buttoned Leona's coat before she put on her own.

The snow was coming down harder and thicker than ever. It was so thick Hattie could barely see the shapes of trees in the schoolyard. Then she heard the crackling sound of tree limbs. The heavy snow was tearing them loose from the trees.

How could a blizzard come up this quickly? thought Hattie. *Only a few hours before, the sun was shining and there was no snow at all.*

The children were silent as they quickly climbed on the bus. They knew how serious a winter blizzard could be. Hattie huddled in her seat. She missed her brother Pierce. Why had he stayed home from school today of all days? Her big brother always knew what to do.

Hattie began to worry as she watched the snow swish against the bus. Little drifts formed in every windowpane. The wind howled and shrieked.

Mr. Henkel, the driver, had a hard time seeing the road ahead and went very slowly. It took a long time to drop off the students at their various homes. Finally the bus was near the Broderick farm. The only children still on the bus were Arnold Best and the Hart children.

Suddenly the bus skidded and swerved. Before Mr. Henkel knew it, the bus was in a ditch, its wheels spinning around and around. He could see that the bus was stuck.

Leona started to cry. "Do we have to stay here? Will we freeze to death?" she asked, tears falling down her cheeks.

Hattie put her arms around Leona and patted her. "No, Leona, it will be all right. Someone will come and rescue us," she said bravely.

Mr. Henkel knew no one would dare to come out in this storm. He turned to his passengers.

"We are very close to the Broderick farm," he announced. "I'll lead the way. Children, grab hands. I'll carry Leona. Clarence, you come next. Hattie and Arnold, you'll be at the end of the line. Everyone hold on to the person in front of you. Before we start, we are going to ask God to help us."

They held hands and Mr. Henkel prayed, "God, we need You. Help us to make it to the Broderick farm. Amen."

As they trudged down the road, it was almost impossible to see. They clung together in the blowing snow, hoping they were going in the right direction. Once Mr. Henkel put Leona down and scraped with his boot until he found gravel. He wanted to be sure they were still on the road.

"I'm freezing," sobbed Leona.

"Me too," cried Clarence.

"Just keep going," said Hattie. "God will help us." Realizing she needed all the prayers she could get, Hattie turned to Arnold. "You pray too, Arnold!"

Snow had gotten into Hattie's boots and her toes felt frozen. Her fingers did too, but she didn't say anything. She had to keep encouraging Clarence and Leona.

"I can't go anymore," cried Leona as she sat down in the snow.

Mr. Henkel picked her up again. "I think we're almost there," he said as he spotted the faint outline of the Broderick's mailbox. They walked a few more minutes; then Hattie and Arnold ran ahead. Mrs. Broderick opened the kitchen door and saw a shivering cluster of children.

"Come in as quick as you can," she said. "I wondered if you got home."

Leona was still wailing and Hattie tried to soothe her. Hattie silently thanked God they had made it to the warm kitchen. Even Clarence was crying. "I didn't know if I could make it," he admitted.

Mrs. Broderick checked cheeks and noses to see if anyone had frostbite. "It's a miracle you're all right," she said as she helped the little ones remove their boots and wraps.

"Come in as quick as you can," she said.

"Let's celebrate," said Mrs. Broderick. "How about some hot cocoa?" She went to get some milk to heat, and soon was passing out cups to everyone.

This hot cocoa tastes so good, thought Hattie. As she sipped her drink, she remembered her parents might be worried that the children hadn't arrived home.

"Can I call Mom and Dad?" asked Hattie.

"The last time I tried to use the phone, the lines were down," said Mrs. Broderick. "You had better stay here tonight."

Meanwhile at home, the Harts were wondering where their children were.

"They must be staying in the schoolhouse overnight. At least they're out of the storm and warm," said Dad. "I'm sure it will let up and we can check on them first thing in the morning."

He turned away quickly so Mom would not see his worried face. He was certain the blizzard would last all night.

"Come on, Pierce. We need to bring in more wood," said Dad. Together they brought in several armloads.

The wind continued to blow fiercely.

By the next morning, it had stopped snowing and the wind had died down. Hattie was staring out the Brodericks' front window, wondering what Mom and Dad were thinking. Suddenly she saw her father and Pierce trudging down the road pulling a toboggan. She was out the door in a flash, waving her arms. "Dad! Dad! We're here!"

All Dad could say was, "Thank God," as he turned in at the Broderick farm. He grabbed Hattie in his arms and held her for a long time.

"God is good. God is good," Hattie said.

Chapter 10

Play Practice in the Parlor

*H*attie was determined to make Christmas last as long as possible. Right after her birthday, Hattie had started saving the silvery wrappers from the gum that John, the hired man, gave her. She used them to fashion icicles for the Christmas tree.

At school Miss Henry helped the class make their own Advent calendars so they could count the days before Christmas. Hattie's class made paper snowflakes that were as pretty as Princess Anne's lace collar. Red-and-green paper chains and construction-paper Christmas trees adorned the classroom.

The class was singing "Up on the Housetop" and "Silent Night." Hattie loved to sing, but she liked being the center of attention even better.

"Miss Henry, may I make up a Christmas play to do in the school program?" Hattie offered one day.

"How nice of you to offer, Hattie," Miss Henry replied. "Why don't you and Ruthie work together? Then you can present your ideas to the class."

Hattie was overjoyed. She knew she was the best writer in class. Her mother said Ruthie could come over that Friday evening to work on the play.

"Hattie," Dad said as he buttoned his overcoat. "Your mother and I are going Christmas shopping. We are leaving Pierce in charge. We expect you and Ruthie to mind him while we're out."

Hattie hated the thought of having to listen to her brother, but she agreed.

"Yes, Dad," she said. Then she stood on her tiptoes and whispered in his ear. "Here's some of my birthday money. Buy Mom a pretty handkerchief for me." She pressed the coins into his hand.

As soon as Mr. and Mrs. Hart were out the door, Pierce took the three younger children upstairs to read a story. Hattie and Ruthie headed straight to the kitchen for cookies and milk.

"Mom won't mind if I borrow two of her fancy teacups for our milk," Hattie said in her most grown-up voice. "After all, she says they're her 'company cups,' and you're company!"

Ruthie loved going to Hattie's house. It was so big and noisy and full of good smells.

"Oh, Hattie, your Christmas tree is ex-exquisite," Ruthie stuttered, trying to use a word she'd heard

74

her mom use.

"Oh, yes, thank you soooo much, dear," Hattie said, speaking in grown-up tones.

Hattie and Ruthie gazed at the tree as they sipped their milk and pretended to have tea. Icicles made from gum wrappers and a popcorn-and-cranberry garland hung from the branches. Mom had crocheted and starched dazzling white snowflakes as a new addition to the other handmade ornaments.

"I like the candles best of all," Ruthie said. "Father says we can't light ours until Christmas Eve. When will you light yours?"

"Christmas Eve, like you," Hattie sighed, wishing she made the rules instead of Dad.

"Let's start on the play," Hattie announced when the girls had eaten their fill of ginger cookies and rich milk.

"First we'll need a baby Jesus," Hattie directed. "We'll use my doll Princess Anne. If we wrap her in a dish towel, no one will know she's a girl."

Hattie took a towel off the tray and carefully placed it around Princess Anne. As she wrapped the doll, she thought of a problem. Should she be Mary, the mother of Jesus, or the Christmas angel? She wasn't sure which part would be the most important.

"May I be Mary?" Ruthie asked suddenly. "I have a pretty blue bathrobe at home that I could wear. And my mother will make something for my head."

"Well, I suppose," Hattie said. "Do you think your mother would make me a halo if I play the Christmas angel?" Hattie asked.

"I'm sure she will," Ruthie offered.

"Then it's settled," Hattie said. She put Anne, now dressed as baby Jesus, under the tree. As she did, Hattie's eyes caught sight of a pretty blue candle near the back of the Christmas tree.

"Ruthie," Hattie said, "check and see what Pierce is doing."

Ruthie peeked around the corner. She couldn't see Pierce, but she could hear him reading stories to the children upstairs.

She came back into the parlor. "He's upstairs, Hattie. What are you going to do?"

"You see this?" Hattie asked as she unclipped the candle holder from its branch. "This will be the light the Christmas angel will hold in the play."

"Are you sure it's okay?" Ruthie questioned. She was starting to feel uncomfortable.

"We won't light it," Hattie said. "I'll just hold it."

Hattie got her dad's Bible and read the Christmas story. She and Ruthie acted out their parts and decided who from their class would be best as Joseph, the shepherds, the three wise men, and the animals.

"Too bad there's no pig in the story," Hattie grinned. "That means Arnold Best won't have a part!"

"I think Arnold would be a good innkeeper," suggested Ruthie kindly.

Soon Hattie became bored with being the angel. "Ruthie, please go into the kitchen and get the matches for me," Hattie asked.

"No," Ruthie said, "please don't light the candle, Hattie. Something awful will happen, I just know it!"

Without a word, Hattie stepped out of the parlor, stole into the kitchen, and grabbed a match. She struck it on the iron stove and carefully cupped her hand around it.

Quick as a wink, she was back in the parlor, lighting that little blue candle. She stuffed the used match into her dress pocket.

Just as she held the candle up majestically, she heard Pierce coming down the stairs. "Hattie," he called, "what are you two doing?"

Ruthie froze, but Hattie blew out the candle and threw it under the tree with the baby Jesus doll. Then Hattie shoved the tray and teacups under the sofa.

Pierce appeared at the door, feeling pleased at the way he was taking care of the house while Mom and Dad were gone.

Hattie glanced nervously at the candle she had tossed under the tree. Then she stared in horror. The

*Ruthie froze, but Hattie blew out the candle
and threw it under the tree.*

tree was on fire! Hattie pushed Ruthie aside and dived for her doll. As she fell into the tree, it toppled over onto the parlor rug. By now, the whole Christmas tree was on fire!

Pierce rushed into the parlor, shielding his face from the heat and flames. He pulled Hattie and Ruthie from the room.

"Get me a blanket! And some water!" Pierce commanded.

Hattie ran to Mom and Dad's bed and pulled off the coverlet with both hands. Pierce covered the tree with the white, embroidered coverlet as Hattie brought water to throw on the tree.

Pierce had the fire out quickly, but Hattie's crying was not doused as easily. Her hair was frizzled on the ends and her face was sooty, but she was not badly hurt.

Ruthie was in shock.

"I'm sorry, I'm sorry," Hattie said over and over.

Pierce looked from one to the other. "You and Ruthie were the last ones in the parlor. Were you playing with matches in there?"

Not wanting to lie, Hattie ignored the question. Then she remembered Princess Anne. She raced into the parlor to find her prized doll. As she pawed through the rubble on her hands and knees, she began to cry again.

"Princess Anne was here," she sobbed. "And now,

she's nothing but ashes!"

Pierce stooped down near Hattie, feeling sorry for her. "Come on, Hattie, go change your clothes. Mom and Dad will be home soon."

As Hattie turned to go upstairs, Pierce noticed a brown spot on the pocket. He reached in and pulled out a blackened match.

"Hattie! You were playing with matches!" he shouted. "And now you've ruined the tree, the parlor rug, and Mom and Dad's coverlet. And think of what could have happened to you!"

"I know. I've ruined everything," she sobbed. "We could have all died! And my precious Princess Anne . . . and—"

"And what?" Pierce questioned.

Hattie hurried back into the parlor to check on the teacups under the sofa. They were exactly as Hattie and Ruthie had placed them. And safe beside them was Dad's Bible that Hattie had used to read the Christmas story.

"Thank goodness these are all right," Hattie said. She then explained to Pierce about the play, the Christmas angel's candle, and how Princess Anne had caught fire. No sooner had the words tumbled from her mouth than Mom and Dad entered the house.

Mom looked as though she would faint, and Dad quickly helped her to bed.

Pierce took Dad aside and explained everything to him. Dad was so grateful that Hattie hadn't been hurt and the house hadn't burned down that he wasn't angry with Hattie. That and the fact that Ruthie hadn't gone home yet, saved Hattie from a spanking right then and there.

"Dad, I'm so sorry about the tree and the mess and your coverlet," she said. "I never, ever meant to hurt anyone."

"I know you didn't mean to do any of those things, Hattie," Dad said. "But once they were done, you shouldn't have lied about it. Not admitting your mistake was your biggest mistake."

Hattie knew he was right.

"I will pray for God to forgive me tonight, Dad."

Dad scooped Hattie up in his arms. "I'm grateful to God it wasn't any worse," he said. "I forgive you, and your mother will too. Right now, we have a mess to clean up. And tomorrow we'll have to get a new tree."

Chapter 11

Lady Loretta Lavender

*W*inter was settling in and the nights were turning bitter cold. Hattie knew there would be no doll for her this Christmas since Princess Anne had burned up in the fire. Mom was too busy sewing a new coverlet for her bed to make a new doll.

Every time Hattie thought about the fire, she shuddered. Even though she knew she was forgiven, she saw flames in her dreams every night.

Mom had patched the hole in the parlor rug, and a new Christmas tree stood almost as tall as the old one. Of course, most of its ornaments weren't as grand as the ones that had burned.

It took a long time to make new garlands. It didn't help that Clarence thought it was more fun to eat the popcorn than to string it. At least nobody ate the raw cranberries.

Hattie and Clarence brought home construction-paper snowflakes they created at school, and Leona helped Pierce put them on the tree. Still Hattie missed the beautiful white ornaments that Mom had so carefully crocheted for the tree.

Ruthie's mother, Mrs. Rhenn, sent over a box of fragile, hand-painted ornaments for the Harts. She felt so bad about the fire—and Ruthie's part in it.

"The Rhenns will not have as many gifts for themselves this year because of what they gave us," Mom said gratefully.

Hattie was grateful too, not just for new ornaments, but for the way everyone was trying to help her family have a blessed Christmas after all.

A week went by before Hattie stopped dreaming about the fire. She awoke on Saturday morning ready for an adventure.

Right before breakfast Dad pulled Hattie and Leona aside and told them a secret. "Dr. Sporrey and his wife are moving away soon, so they are having an auction at their house today," he whispered. "I want you two to go with me and see if there's a dresser your mother would like for Christmas."

Hattie raced through breakfast and the dishes so she could go with Dad on his secret journey. He told Mom he was going to Dr. Sporrey's to get some medicine for Ervin—which was true. He didn't say anything about the dresser.

The two Hart girls loved going places with their

dad. He always introduced them to people they met just like they were grown-up ladies.

Hattie practiced curtsying in the bedroom.

"Why are you doing that?" her little sister asked.

"You never know. Today we may meet a princess, or even a queen, on our secret journey," Hattie said as she dipped to the floor.

Leona's eyes grew big. "Are you teasing me, Hattie?" she asked.

The girls raced downstairs, grabbed their coats, and tumbled into Dad's Model-T Ford.

As the car jiggled and clunked down the bumpy road, Hattie and Leona looked out the window at the gleaming snow. It clung to every tree branch.

"I'm so glad it snowed last night," Hattie said out loud. "I love the way the snow sticks to the tree branches and makes the bushes look like big popcorn balls."

Dad didn't say much as he drove, but just being out with him on such a glorious winter day inspired Hattie to make up a little poem.

"Listen to this," she said.

I see the snow
In the month of December.
The sparkle and glitter
I want to remember.

"That's very nice, Hattie," Dad remarked. "God gave you a talent with words."

Hattie tried to make up another poem, but she couldn't think of any more rhymes. She went back to looking out the window until they arrived at Dr. Sporrey's house.

"Here we are," Dad announced. Hattie was surprised at the empty yard. No one else had come to the auction.

"Dr. Sporrey offered to let us take a look at the furniture before the auction starts," Dad explained.

Mr. Hart, Hattie, and Leona stomped the snow from their feet at the door. When it opened, they stepped into the most beautiful house Hattie had ever seen.

Mrs. Sporrey greeted them warmly, and offered to make some cocoa.

"None for me," Dad said. "But I'm sure my girls would like some. You know my daughters, Hattie and Leona, don't you, Mrs. Sporrey?"

"Oh, yes," she said. "My, what lovely ladies they've become."

Hattie smiled and tried to curtsy, but her foot caught under the parlor rug and she thumped down on the bare wood floor.

Dr. Sporrey, who had just entered the room, helped Hattie to her feet. Then he inspected the floor.

"No, she didn't make a hole in it!" Dr. Sporrey

laughed. He had a large, round face and his cheeks were always bright red. He laughed a lot, and Hattie was glad!

Dr. Sporrey led the three Harts up the long, winding staircase. As they reached the doorway to the Sporreys' bedroom, Hattie gasped with delight.

"It's beautiful!" she said.

"Yes, it is a handsome piece of furniture," Dad replied.

"No!" cried Hattie. "I mean that!"

Hattie wasn't looking at the dresser. She was gazing at a delicate figure on the bed.

"That doll is the prettiest doll on earth. She's even prettier than Princess Anne," Hattie whispered under her breath.

"Oh, that belongs to my wife," explained Dr. Sporrey. "They gave it to her last year at the church—for all her help at the church bazaars."

"I love her," Hattie said, wishing she could stroke the doll's blonde hair or touch its purple velvet dress.

"Now, Hattie," Dad interrupted. "We're here to look at a dresser. We don't have money to buy a new doll."

Hattie, Leona, and Dad all agreed that the dresser was perfect for Mom. It had a large mirror and delicate carvings around the drawers. And it was big, so big that John, the hired man, would have to come for it in the wagon.

Hattie listened while Dad and Dr. Sporrey discussed the price for the dresser, but she couldn't take her eyes off the beautiful doll.

"I was right," Hattie whispered to the lace-collared doll. "I did meet a princess today!"

Soon the dresser deal was made and the cocoa was ready. Mrs. Sporrey gave Leona an enamel cup, but Hattie sipped hot chocolate from a fine china cup like the grown-ups. She was very careful not to bang her cup on the delicate saucer.

As they drank, Dr. Sporrey whispered something in his wife's ear, and she disappeared.

After finishing the cocoa and biscuits with jam, the Harts climbed back into their car. People were outside, waiting for the auction to begin. Hattie was sorry the Sporreys were moving, but she was glad Dad had bought the dresser to remind them of the kind doctor and his wife.

Just as Dad was about to pull away, Mrs. Sporrey ran from the house, waving wildly for Dad to stop. She had something in each hand, but Hattie couldn't tell what. As she walked closer to the car, Hattie recognized the purple dress and squealed with delight.

"Here you are," Mrs. Sporrey said as she handed the doll to Hattie. "I didn't know what I was going to do with this doll. No reason for her to be wasted on an old doctor's wife!"

"Thank you! Thank you!" Hattie said. She was so excited she almost jumped from the car to hug Mrs. Sporrey. "Oh, thank you!" she said again. "I will take such good care of her, and I will remember you forever for giving her to me."

Then Mrs. Sporrey turned to Leona.

"I bought this hand mirror for my niece's birthday, but it turned out she had one just like it," she told Leona. "I thought you might like it."

Leona clasped the mirror with both hands. "Oh, it's beautiful. Thank you so much!" she said.

"I don't know," Dad began. The girls held their breath. They knew their father was a proud man and it was hard for him to accept gifts, even for his daughters.

"Didn't you know?" Mrs. Sporrey broke in. "They are free gifts with the purchase of a dresser!"

Dad smiled. When he thanked Mrs. Sporrey, Hattie knew the doll truly was hers.

On the way home, Hattie didn't gaze out the window or make up poems. She stared at her new doll and touched her velvet dress and curly blonde hair.

"I have to name her. What do you think I should call her?" she asked Dad.

"How about Lady?" Dad offered.

"Lady," Hattie rolled the title off her tongue. "I

like that," Hattie smiled. "Lady . . . Lady Loretta. Lady Loretta Lavender! Yes, that's perfect."

Chapter 12

Christmas Poems for Everyone

*H*attie looked at all the presents under the tree. The neighbors had given the Harts many gifts since their first Christmas tree had burned. Hattie picked up a present with her name on it. She shook it. She smelled it. She ripped a tiny bit of paper off one corner, but she couldn't guess what it might be.

"Please," said Mom, when she caught Hattie checking her present, "you are worse than the little ones. Ach, what can you do with so much curiosity?"

"I was only dusting the presents." Hattie said the first thing that popped into her head. Quickly she started swishing the dust cloth.

"Hattie Marie Hart! Those presents haven't been under the tree long enough to gather dust," Mom exclaimed. "Please leave them alone. You handle the packages so much, they look like they were wrapped in last year's paper."

Hattie didn't think that was true. The presents were all wrapped in this year's newspaper. Besides, the dates were on them. It would cost too much money to use fancy paper. But Mom was right about one thing—patience was not one of Hattie's virtues.

Christmas Eve finally arrived. Mom's great Christmas supper was first. She had cooked thick slices of ham and fried chicken, fresh doughnuts, and biscuits with peach jelly.

"Hurry with the dishes," said Clarence, "so Dad can read the Christmas story. Then we can open our presents."

Hattie never got tired of hearing the Christmas story. Dad read it from *Egermeier's Bible Story Book.* Even little Ervin sat still and listened.

"Can we have our presents now?" asked Leona.

"Let Ervin be first," said Mom. "It's hard for the him to wait." Soon Ervin was happily rolling a new red ball to Pierce.

Leona opened two presents. They were both small—a jump rope and barrettes. She said "thank you" so nicely to Mom and Dad that everyone remembered to say thank you, too.

Finally it was time for the older children to open their presents. Hattie, Pierce, and Clarence had made up poems for one another to go with their presents. Making Christmas poems was something Dad had done as a boy in Holland, and Hattie was glad they had kept up the custom.

With Hattie's help, Clarence had written a poem for Pierce's present.

> *Merrily you will skate on these*
> *But if you fall you'll hurt your knees.*
> *So get right up or you will freeze.*

The present was a new pair of skates. "Thanks a lot, folks," said Pierce with a big grin.

Hattie couldn't believe she was the last one to open a present. She quickly read the poem Pierce had written:

> *It isn't books or shoes or socks*
> *That you will find inside this box.*
> *It's something that goes stitch-stitchie.*
> *I hope you like it, little Hitchie.*

Hitchie was a nickname that Hattie hated, but she was anxious to find out what was in the package. Rip! went the paper as Hattie tore into the box. There before her was a present so special she could have never imagined she would own such a thing— a miniature sewing machine!

"This is just like Mom's," said Hattie. She was so

She quickly read the poem Pierce had written.

excited. She would be able to take it anywhere, anytime, and sew whatever she wanted.

Christmas morning came at last. During the night eight inches of new snow had fallen. Right after breakfast, Dad and Pierce carried the handsome dresser from the Sporreys into the house. Mom was so happy that she hugged Dad right in front of everyone! "You are too kind, too kind," she said.

There was so much snow that Dad couldn't use the car to take the family to church. Instead, he hitched up the horses to the bobsled. They snorted as he snapped the whip to urge them forward.

Hattie snuggled down in mounds of golden, sweet-smelling straw and covered herself with blankets. Mom had placed hot bricks wrapped in cloths down in the sled, near the children's toes.

Even before Hattie saw the little white church in the distance, she heard the singing of Dutch hymns and carols through the tree branches.

Away in a manger,
No crib for a bed,
The little Lord Jesus
Lay down His sweet head.

"Listen, Mom," said Hattie. "They're singing a Christmas poem for Jesus. Let's hurry so we can sing too!"

Experience the *Treasures of Childhood*
Growing up in a twelve-member family on a farm in the
1920s creates many opportunities for adventure and
discovery. Enjoy each exciting book in the *Treasures of
Childhood* series as young Hattie Hart explores the
magnificent world around her and learns important
value lessons in the process.

Meet Hattie
Hattie has a difficult time obeying the simple rules on her
family's farm. Whether she's stretching the truth to sell
seeds or breaking Mom's best candy dish, each new day
teaches her the value of her family's love.

Hattie's Faraway Family
Hattie volunteers to drive Mrs. Lynn to Worthington—
even though she's never driven before. Then, baby Elmer
disappears at the beach when she is suppose to be
watching him. These adventures and others teach Hattie
the importance of responsibility.

Hattie's Adventures
Her best friend gets stranded on the roof when Hattie
and her brothers take away the ladder she used to get up.
Then, Hattie thinks up a dirty trick to get even with her
brother for a prank he pulled on her. Through all the
teasing, they learn to laugh together and appreciate each
other.

Each title is available at your favorite Christian bookstore.